For our family

— C.C. and S.O.

Produced exclusively for Little Souls, Inc.
by Chronicle Books LLC.

Chronicle Books LLC
85 Second Street
San Francisco, California 94105

Art direction and book design
by Vandy Ritter.

Typeset in Weiss and Ballerino.
The illustrations in this book were rendered
in watercolor, acrylic and cut paper collage.

Printed in Hong Kong.

ISBN 0-8118-2864-6

10 9 8 7 6 5 4 3 2 1

# One Enchanted Christmas

## A LITTLE SOULS® TALE

by Colleen Charleston

illustrated by Sally Onopa

*O*nce upon a time, there was an old Victorian house that was home to two elderly sisters and one aging Siamese cat. Out of a small front room these sisters ran a busy hat and dress shop, from which they supplied the fanciest department stores in the city.

Third Avenue

Francesca, the dressmaker, was a gentle woman who raised her children in this very house, and who now enjoyed the visits from her many grandchildren. She wore layers of brightly colored satin jackets, exotic jewelry and comfortable shoes. Her gray hair was piled high and held in place by a confusion of chopsticks, hat pins, sewing supplies, reading glasses and a splendid recipe for salsa.

$\mathcal{H}$er sister Tori was the hatmaker, whose creations were known for their unexpected details: a silver spoon, a china tea cup nestled in mounds of bows, flowers, ostrich plumes and beaded fruit. Tori often wore strappy heels, and when designing her fantastic hats, she would dramatically wrap herself in yards of brilliant silk (or, on one occasion, the dining room tablecloth).

Holidays were especially magical at the sisters' house. The comings and goings of family and friends stirred about the workshop's feathers, bits of fabric, lace and ribbon, causing them to drift down in a glittering confetti as if to bless the house, and all who entered there.

One Christmas Eve, Isa, Francesca's youngest grandchild, came to visit. Isa could not have asked for a better place to play dress-up than the little front room where her grandmother worked.

Splendid
Salsa
4 C. tomatoes
2 cloves garlic
1 red pepper
2 T. cilantro
1 onion

She particularly loved the heavy, red velvet drapes.
The lengths of fabric had given generations of
children an enchanted place in which to imagine.

    Dreams came easily to Isa while she hid
in the velvet's deep folds.

$\mathcal{A}$s Grandmother and Great Aunt hurried about the workshop's clutter, putting last-minute touches on their dresses and hats, Isa wrapped herself in the warmth of the drapery and watched them. Spying Isa's hiding place, Francesca beckoned her granddaughter to a footstool.

"It's time to replace those curtains! Let's make you something special to wear on Christmas day!"

*I*sa was startled to see her grandmother snip apart one of the curtains and quickly cut and stitch it into a coat. Aunt Tori fashioned a wonderful matching hat. Then Tori bent and whispered in Isa's ear,

"You know, child, your grandmother has sewn only one other creation like this. It was made years ago for a very special client—a kind old gentleman who also loves red velvet. This coat, too, is special because it is made with the fabric of your dreams."

*I*ndeed, the velvet, which had darkened with age, now glowed on Isa. Several half-moon pockets for Isa's treasures and small hands were sewn on either side. And inside, next to her heart, was another tiny pocket.

"Keep the pockets filled—you never know when you will need the gifts they hold," Tori added.

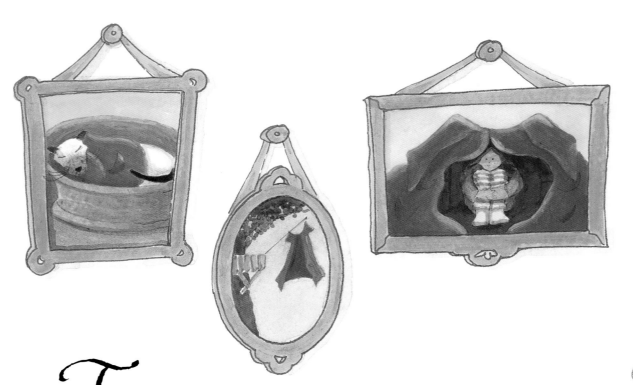

That night, when Tori and Francesca tucked Isa into bed, the coat was still wrapped tightly around her. It had the unmistakable scent of the house and of the people she adored.

Over the next year, Isa's red coat became a much-loved dolly's blanket, a treehouse flag and the roof of a simple fort. Eventually it found a home, slung over a bedpost, never far from Isa's tousled head.

There, its pockets held the treasures that Isa held dear: a locket from a best friend, beach glass that flashed the color blue, an iridescent butterfly wing, trinkets like those used in Tori's hats. Memories of places, people adored. With the daily addition of each simple blessing, the coat quietly grew.

$\mathcal{T}$he approach of Christmas
once again found the two sisters
happily working on their special
creations. There were last-minute
requests for sequins and stars, boas
and rhinestones.

$\mathcal{L}$ate on Christmas Eve, as the last satisfied customers left, and the shop was about to close, a large, flustered looking gentleman stepped in. The two sisters recognized him at once as the jolly old fellow who had long ago purchased the rather distinctive red velvet suit.

"Ladies, ladies," he boomed in a deep voice, and with a twinkle in his eye. "I'm in a pickle and require your assistance. I've just begun my trip, but have already ruined my coat, and only a tree limb knows where my hat is. Please, my wife insists that I must wear a coat tonight, or I'll catch my death by cold. Could you quickly make me a new one?"

From her favorite spot behind the curtain, Isa watched as Grandmother and Great Aunt sadly shook their heads no. They wanted to help, but it was too late. They couldn't possibly fashion a hat and coat of such grand dimensions in time. Seeing the old man's disappointment, Isa had an idea and quietly slipped out the door.

As the customer turned to leave, Isa reappeared and pushed a wrapped bundle toward the kind gentleman.

"What is this, little one? A gift for me? Now that's a twist!

$\mathcal{H}$is rosy cheeks grew rosier still as he gingerly peeled back the wrapping. Spread before them was Isa's coat; once tiny, it had grown in magnificence and proportion. And there, tucked into its many pockets, peeking out from the many deep folds, appeared an abundance of extraordinary gifts.

The old man held the coat to his face and breathed in the fullness of a child's heart. His eyes glistened with thanks. He knelt as the sisters lifted the great coat around his shoulders. Isa tucked a note into the pocket nearest his heart. The man left quickly, laughing with delight.

$I$sa, Francesca and Tori closed the small front room and climbed the stairs to the very top floor. Together they pulled open the moon-shaped window, and there, amongst the glittering stars, watched the sky for the arrival of Father Christmas.